Karen's Sleigh Ride

Little Sister

Karen's Sleigh Ride
Ann M. Martin

Illustrations by Susan Tang

A
LITTLE APPLE
PAPERBACK

SCHOLASTIC INC.
New York Toronto London Auckland Sydney

ISBN 0-590-06590-4

12 11 10 9 8 7 6 5 4 3 2 1   7 8 9/9 0 1 2/0

Printed in the U.S.A.

First Scholastic printing, December 1997   40

The author gratefully acknowledges
Gabrielle Charbonnet
for her help
with this book.

Karen's Sleigh Ride

Christmas Is in the Air

"Please pass the glue," said Hannie Papadakis.

I was twisting pipe cleaners into the shape of an angel, but I put it down long enough to pass her the glue.

"Where are the gold sprinkles?" asked Andrew.

"Right here," said Hannie. She gave him the jar.

I twisted the last pipe cleaner into place. "There!" I said. "One more angel."

You might be wondering who we are and

what we were doing. Well, I am Karen Brewer. I am seven years old. Andrew is my little brother. He is four going on five. And Hannie is one of my best friends. (I have two.)

We were sitting around the kitchen table at the big house. (I have two houses — a big house and a little house. I will tell you more about them later.) We were making Christmas decorations. Even though it was only the second day of December, I wanted to start preparing for Christmas. You cannot leave everything until the last minute.

Another reason we were inside that afternoon was because it was snowing very hard. It was snowing so hard that we could not play outside. Snow is one of the things you have to deal with when you live in Stoneybrook, Connecticut. It is a good thing that I love snow. I also love December, and Christmas.

"More goo!" said Emily Michelle. Emily is my little sister. She was sitting in her high chair next to the kitchen table. (She is only

2

two and a half years old.) We had given her some construction-paper shapes and a little bit of glue. She was making her own decorations.

"Okay. You may have a tiny bit more glue," said Nannie. Nannie is my step-grandmother. She lives with us at the big house and helps take care of everyone.

"I cannot believe we have to wait twenty-three more days until Christmas," said Hannie. She sprinkled some green glitter onto her red construction paper.

"Twenty-three days will take forever," said Andrew. He was making white snowflakes to tape to our windows.

"We will just have to keep busy," I said. "We have twenty-three days to make this the best Christmas ever. That is plenty of time." Then I had a neat idea. "Hey! I know! Let's decide to do something Christmassy every single day, from now until Christmas."

"Like what?" asked Andrew.

"Like, each day we will sing Christmas

4

carols," I said. "Or wrap presents. Or make Christmas cookies. Or make Christmas decorations. Or read Christmas books." I was very excited about my idea.

Hannie smiled. "That will be fun. And we have to do something Christmassy every day whether we are together or not."

Emily had been listening to us. "Pwesants!" she cried. She waved her hands in the air. "Pwesants!" She looked at Nannie.

"Yes, honey," said Nannie. "When Christmas comes, you will get some presents."

"On Christmas, Santa Claus brings presents to all the good boys and girls," I said. It is part of my job as a big sister to teach Emily Michelle (and Andrew) about all kinds of stuff.

"You better watch out," sang Hannie. "You better not cry."

Andrew and I started singing too. "You better not pout, I'm telling you why. Santa Claus is coming to towwwwwn."

After that song, we tried to teach Emily more Christmas songs.

"Jingle bells," I sang. "Jingle bells, jingle all the waaay. Oh, what fun it is to ride in a one-horse open sleigh, hey!"

"Jimble bells," sang Emily Michelle. "Jimble bells!"

I could not help laughing. Christmas was coming, and that made me happy. And Emily is so funny sometimes. I was very glad she had come to live with us. Now I had better explain everything about the big house and little house and Nannie and Emily Michelle.

Karen's Two Houses

A long time ago, when I was little, Andrew and I lived in the big house all the time. Back then the people in my family were Andrew, Mommy, Daddy, and me. Then Mommy and Daddy decided to get a divorce. So Mommy took Andrew and me to live with her in the little house. (Daddy stayed in the big house. It is where he grew up.) Then Mommy got married again, to a very nice man named Seth Engle. So Seth is my stepfather. Nowadays at the little house are Mommy, Seth, Andrew, and me. There are also Midgie, Seth's dog, and Rocky, Seth's cat. Not to mention Bob, Andrew's pet hermit crab, and Emily Junior, my pet rat. (I named her after Emily Michelle.)

Daddy also got married again, to Elizabeth Thomas. So Elizabeth is my stepmother. She already had four kids, and they are my stepbrothers and stepsister. Sam and Charlie are so old that they are in high school. David Michael is seven like me, but he does not go to my school. Kristy is thirteen, and the best big sister ever. Then Daddy and Elizabeth adopted Emily Michelle. She was born in a faraway country called Vietnam.

After Emily arrived, Nannie, who is Elizabeth's mother, came to live with us. Besides all the people, Nannie helps take care of Shannon, who is David Michael's gigundo puppy, Boo-Boo, who is Daddy's cat (Boo-Boo is old and cranky and not much fun), and Goldfishie and Crystal Light the second, who are (guess what) goldfish.

Now Andrew and I spend one month at

the little house and one month at the big house. (Emily Junior and Bob go back and forth with us.) We just had Thanksgiving at the little house. Now we would have Christmas at the big house. I am very glad I have two houses and two families to care for me.

You know what? I have two of a lot of things. In fact, I call myself Karen Two-Two sometimes. I have two houses, and two families, two stuffed cats (one at each house), and two bicycles (one at each house). I even wear two pairs of glasses. The blue ones are for reading, and the pink ones are for the rest of the time. And I already told you I have two best friends. Hannie lives across the street and one house down from the big house. Nancy Dawes lives next door to the little house. Together, Nancy and Hannie and I are the Three Musketeers.

Most of the time I like being a Two-Two. Sometimes it is a little tiring.

Today I was very happy to be at the big house with my big-house family.

"Hey, what are you guys doing?" Kristy came into the kitchen. Her nose and cheeks were red from the cold.

"Making Christmas decorations," I said, holding one up.

"Terrific," said Kristy. "They will make the house look very Christmassy."

I smiled. Kristy is nice.

"Did you hear the sad news?" asked Kristy. "There was a fire last night. Mr. and Mrs. Stone's barn burned down."

"Oh, no," I said. I covered my mouth with my hand. Mr. and Mrs. Stone own a farm at the edge of town. In the summers Mrs. Stone runs a farm camp. I went to it with Hannie and Nancy. It was really fun. Kristy was one of our counselors.

"How awful for the Stones," said Nannie. "Was anyone hurt?"

Kristy shook her head. "No. No one was in the barn."

"What about the animals?" I cried. "Were any animals hurt in the fire?" I had fallen in love with a lamb named Ollie there. All of

Mrs. Stone's animals were adorable. I could not bear it if any of them had gotten hurt.

"No, do not worry," said Kristy. "The firemen and the Stones managed to save all of the animals. They were very lucky."

"Thank heavens," I said. "But poor Mr. and Mrs. Stone."

"What a shame," said Nannie.

"Yes, it sure is," agreed Kristy.

I looked down at our beautiful Christmas decorations, lying on the table. I did not feel quite as happy as before.

Mrs. Stone's Barn

There are so many of us at the big house that we eat our meals at a long, long table with two long, long benches. I usually try to sit next to Kristy.

Tonight we were having pot roast with vegetables. Yum!

After everyone had passed their plates around and had been served, I tapped my water glass.

"Ahem!" I said. "Daddy, did you hear about Mrs. Stone's barn?"

"Yes, I did," said Daddy. "It is too bad.

They are not sure how the fire started."

"It is a good thing it happened in winter, when there is snow on the ground and on the trees," said Elizabeth. "The snow helped keep everything else from burning too."

"Does this mean that Mrs. Stone will not be able to have farm camp next summer?" I asked.

"I do not know about next summer's farm camp," said Daddy. "But the Stones will probably rebuild their barn."

"Where are the animals staying now?" I asked. "They need to be someplace warm. It is freezing outside."

No one knew.

I looked out the kitchen window. It was still snowing. A cold wind was blowing. I thought about poor little Ollie. And Elvira the goat.

"We have to find out what has happened to the animals," I said. "I would not mind sharing my room with Ollie, if he needs a place to stay."

Daddy smiled at me. "I do not think Ollie

would be very happy staying in your room," he said. "But it is a nice offer. I'll tell you what. Tomorrow I will call Mrs. Stone and find out about the animals, okay? I am sure they are being taken care of."

"That is a good idea," said Elizabeth. "When you call her, could you please ask if they need help in any way?"

"I will," promised Daddy.

"I know!" I cried. I had just had *another* good idea. "We could have a barn raising for them! I saw a TV show about one once. We could bring food, and everyone would pitch in and build them a new barn."

"Um, I am not sure I am up to building a new barn," said Daddy. "But I will call and find out if we can help the Stones somehow."

"Okay," I said. I felt disappointed. The barn raising had looked like so much fun on TV. But I would just have to wait for Daddy to find out what we needed to do.

In her high chair Emily Michelle waved her spoon. "You bedda washout," she sang.

Elizabeth smiled at her and wiped off her chin. (Emily is a messy eater.) "You are so excited about Christmas, aren't you?" said Elizabeth.

"Pwesants?" asked Emily Michelle. She looked under her high chair.

"Not yet, silly," said Andrew. "No presents for twenty-three days."

I look a bite of carrot. Christmas was twenty-three days away. I knew our Christmas would be wonderful here at the big house. But what would Christmas be like for the Stones this year?

We Need a Plan

"How was school today, honey?" Elizabeth asked me. It was the next evening. I was helping Elizabeth set the table for dinner.

"Wonderful," I said. School usually is wonderful. That is because I have the best teacher in the world, Ms. Colman. "Today we started to learn about winter holidays around the world. We are learning about Christmas in other countries, plus Hanukkah and Kwanzaa."

"It sounds very interesting," said Elizabeth. "And it reminds me that I need to start shopping soon for Christmas presents."

"I already know what I am getting for everyone in my two families," I said. "I have been thinking about it a lot. And I have been saving my money."

"Good for you," said Elizabeth.

Actually, after all my thinking, I still did not know what to get Hannie for Christmas and Nancy for Hanukkah. I wanted to think of the perfect gifts. I would have to work on it.

"Santa!" Emily Michelle shouted, running into the kitchen. "Pwesants!"

"Emily, you have Christmas on the brain," I said.

"She needs to relax about Christmas," said Kristy, following Emily into the room. "She is making me crazy."

"Jimble bells, jimble bells," sang Emily. She marched around the room, singing. I tried not to listen. Instead, I watched the rest of my family wander into the kitchen.

18

When we were all sitting down, Daddy said, "I talked to Mr. Stone today."

"Oh, goody!" I said. "How are all the animals? Where are they? Are the Stones all right? Do they need me to keep Ollie in my room for awhile?"

Daddy held up his hand. "Hold on a minute, Karen. One question at a time. The animals are fine. For the moment they are staying in some smaller buildings on the property, but they will need better lodgings soon. Ollie does not need to stay in your room, though."

Across the table Sam snickered. I ignored him.

"However," continued Daddy, "the Stones do need some help. It turns out that they did not keep their fire insurance up-to-date. So the money the insurance company is giving them is not nearly enough to rebuild their barn."

"Uh-oh," said David Michael. "What are they going to do?"

"Well, there is not much they can do,"

said Daddy. "They could sell off their animals, so they would not need a barn. Or they can sell the farm, and move to a smaller farm somewhere else."

"But that farm has been in Mr. Stone's family for generations," said Kristy. "I heard him say so."

"They cannot sell all their animals," I said. "How would they have a farm camp next summer?"

Daddy shrugged. "They will not have much choice, I'm afraid. Rebuilding a barn like that is very expensive. They simply do not have the money."

"This is terrible," I said. "And right at Christmastime too. They will have an awful Christmas."

"Cwismas!" said Emily Michelle. She wiggled in her high chair. "Cwismas! Jimble bells! Pwesants!"

Kristy sighed. "Could you try *not* to say that word for awhile?" she asked me.

"Sorry," I said. "I am just upset."

"I am upset too," said Kristy. "I love the

Stones. And I loved being a counselor at Mrs. Stone's farm camp. But I do not know what we can do."

"We *have* to do something," I said firmly. "So we will think about it, and we will come up with something." Daddy says sometimes all you need is positive thinking. I was trying to have positive thoughts.

"Okay," said Kristy. "We will try to think of something."

I started eating my dinner quickly. The sooner I finished, the sooner I could start solving the Stones' problem.

The Brilliant Idea

After dinner Kristy and I went into her room. Kristy sat down at her desk. She took out a pad of paper and a pen.

"We will write down all our ideas," she said. "Then we will decide if any of them will work."

"Okay," I said. "Let's see . . . we need to help the Stones. I know! We can turn our garage into a little barn. Then we can keep Ollie and Elvira and maybe one of the horses. That will help the Stones."

"We need a way to help the Stones rebuild *their* barn," Kristy pointed out. "I am sure they do not want all their animals to go to different places. How would they run their farm camp if the animals were all over Stoneybrook?"

"Oh," I said. "Okay. Let me think." I swung my legs against Kristy's bed. She chewed on the end of her pencil. We were thinking so hard, I could almost hear it.

"We could sell candy," I said finally. "I have done that before."

"That is a good idea," said Kristy. "But I am not sure that we could sell enough candy to build a whole barn."

"How about a food drive?" I said. "I have done that before too."

"The Stones do not need food," said Kristy. "They need a new barn."

"An ice-skating show? We raised some money doing that," I said.

"You are coming up with a lot of good ideas," said Kristy. "It is just that we need so *much* money. But keep trying."

I lay back on Kristy's bed. I wiggled my

eyebrows and made faces. I kicked my feet up and down. I hummed a little bit. I was trying to think, think, think.

"I just cannot come up with anything," said Kristy. "I am at the end of my rope."

Kristy's door opened, and Emily Michelle came in. "Hi," she said cheerfully. She opened Kristy's closet door. She peered inside. Then she moved to the dresser and started opening drawers.

"What are you doing?" asked Kristy.

"Santa," said Emily. "Pwesants!"

"Emily," I said, "we have told you a gazillion times. It is not time for Santa Claus yet. It is not time for Christmas yet."

Kristy took Emily Michelle's hand and led her away from the dresser. "There are no presents in there, Emily," she said. "You are just going to have to wait."

Emily started to turn on her "I am about to cry" face.

I jumped up. "I know! Why don't you go to the playroom. I think Andrew is in there. Maybe he will read you a book." Even though Andrew is only four going on five, he knows how to read. I taught him myself. I also taught him to ride a two-wheel bicycle. He is very smart.

Gently I nudged Emily Michelle toward the door. Kristy and I were doing some very important thinking. We could not be bothered with a little kid.

"Jimble bells," Emily started singing. "Jimble bells. One horse open sway, hey!"

"No, Emily," said Kristy, laughing. "It is 'one-horse open *sleigh*.' A *sleigh*. Okay?"

"Okay," said Emily.

I stood up straight. I put my hand to my mouth. "Oh my gosh," I said. "I have an idea! It is perfect! It is gigundoly brilliant! It will solve all the Stones' problems!"

The One-Horse Open Sleigh

"**F**amily meeting!" I yelled. I ran through the hall. "Family meeting! Come on, everyone! In the kitchen!"

Five minutes later my whole big-house family was gathered around the kitchen table. (Except for Nannie, who had decided to give Emily Michelle a bath.)

Kristy tapped her pencil against the tabletop. "Please come to order," she said. I smiled at her. Kristy is so organized. All right," Kristy said. "Karen?"

I stood up. "I have had a gigundoly brilliant idea," I said. "Even more brilliant than a lot of my brilliant ideas."

"Cut to the chase," said Charlie.

I gave him a Look. "My idea is that we have a wintery sort of Christmas party for the Stones, to raise money. We could have games to play and refreshments to buy. But best of all, we would have sleigh rides — in a one-horse open sleigh!" I beamed at my family. They looked back at me.

"Sleigh rides?" asked Elizabeth.

"Yes," I said. "During farm camp I saw an old sleigh in the back of the Stones' little barn, the one that did not burn down. We can dust it off and use it. The Stones' horse can pull it. It has been snowing so much lately. So the horse can pull the sleigh over the snow. And we can charge money. And give the money to the Stones to rebuild their barn. Ta-daaa!"

"Hmm," said Daddy. "I have always wanted to go on a sleigh ride."

"I bet a lot of other people have too," said Kristy. "But the sleigh ride would not have to be the only attraction. We could have lots of fun things for people to do — a winter festival, right at the Stones'. We could have a snowman-building contest. And an ice-sculpting contest."

"We could skate on the Stones' pond," said David Michael. "That would be fun."

"I think this is a great idea," said Elizabeth. "I like having it on the Stones' property. That way they will feel like they are taking part, instead of taking charity. We should talk to the Stones right away."

"It is a terrific idea," said Daddy. "What can we do to help?"

"I could check the sleigh to see if we can really use it," said Sam.

Kristy wrote that down on her pad of paper.

"I could help during the sleigh rides," said Charlie.

Kristy wrote down, *Charlie — help with rides.*

"I could play music for people to skate to," said David Michael. "If I borrow Charlie's boom box."

Kristy made a note. "I am sure he will lend it to you," she said. Charlie nodded.

"You know, Mrs. Stone and I are on the board at the library," said Elizabeth. "I bet the other board members would be happy to help out. I will ask them."

"Maybe I could help advertise the festival," said Daddy. "And I could help build booths or something."

"What about me?" asked Andrew. "What can I do? I need a job."

"You can help me decorate the sleigh," I said. "And make other decorations to put around the farm. You are good at that."

Andrew smiled.

"Good," said Kristy. "I think we all have something to do. We can ask other people if they would like to help too. Everyone knows the Stones. I am sure lots of people will want to get involved."

Daddy put his arm around me. "I am proud of you, Karen," he said. "You too, Kristy. You are doing a good thing for our friends."

I smiled. I liked the Stones, and I was very glad to be able to help them. Best of all, my whole family was helping too. Maybe this would be a good Christmas for the Stones after all!

Karen's Plan

The Stones' winter-festival idea got very big, very fast, very soon. First of all, Daddy took Kristy and me to the Stones' farm to talk to them about it. I felt very sad seeing the empty, burned-out shell where their barn used to be.

But Mr. and Mrs. Stone were happy to hear my idea. They had to think about it a little, but they decided that they would like to hold the festival.

"I think old General Sherman could manage to pull the sleigh," said Mr. Stone. (General Sherman is one of their horses.) "And if he got tired, maybe Ike could take a turn." (Ike is another one of their horses.)

"I will help in any way I can," said Mrs. Stone. "We cannot thank you enough for your wonderful idea."

After that, Elizabeth asked people on the library board to help. They decided to take care of all the refreshments. One man said he would donate hot chocolate. Someone else said she would make doughnuts and cookies. People also signed up to bring hot apple cider, caramel popcorn, and other good things to eat.

Kristy kept track of everything in her notebook.

I asked everyone in Ms. Colman's class to help too. One day during show-and-share time I stood in front of the class. I told everyone about our winter festival.

"It will be wonderful," I told them. "We will try to earn enough money to rebuild the Stones' barn. Does anyone here want to help?"

Right away Hannie and Nancy raised their hands. That is because we are best friends. Best friends always help each other. I smiled at them.

Ms. Colman stepped forward. "What do you need people to do, Karen?"

I was ready for that question. "We still need lots of decorations," I said. "And we need posters telling people about the winter festival. We can hang those around town. Like in stores and stuff."

"I think this would be a good class project," said Ms. Colman. "With all of us working together, we can make lovely decorations and posters. Class, let's take a vote. All those in favor of making decorations for the Stones' winter festival, please raise your hands."

Everyone in my class raised his or her hand!

"It is a great idea," said Addie Sidney.

"I already know what I want to make," said Chris Lamar.

"I went to farm camp there once," said Bobby Gianelli.

"Good, class," said Ms. Colman. "I like your holiday spirit. For the next two weeks we will work on winter-festival decorations and posters during art period. Now it is time for spelling. Please take out your spelling books and your worksheets."

One week later my sleigh-ride idea had turned into a fabulous winter festival. Kristy had asked local stores to donate prizes for the snowman-building contest and the ice-sculpting contest. My class was working on decorations. Elizabeth had put up signs at the library and at her office so that people could donate things or offer to help. There were still tons of things to do, but we were on our way.

I had one important problem left, though: What could I give Hannie for Christmas and Nancy for Hanukkah? I had already made them friendship bracelets. What else would be special? I looked through my arts-and-crafts books for ideas. Hmm. I could make pencil holders out of orange-juice cans. Or I could make bookmarks out of cardboard and fabric. Or I could buy plastic headbands and decorate them.

I sighed. None of these ideas seemed good enough. I needed something extra special for the other two Musketeers. They were my very best friends. But I was stumped. Oh, well. I put away my arts-and-crafts books. I had two more weeks. I was sure I could think of the perfect gifts before then.

First Things First

When I walked into the kitchen a few days later, Kristy was on the phone.

"Yes, that's right," she was saying. "It would just be for a little while. Uh-huh. Do you want to ask your dad? Okay, I'll hold on."

I poured myself a glass of juice. Kristy put the phone on her shoulder. "I am talking to Mary Anne," she told me. (Mary Anne Spier is one of Kristy's friends. She is in the baby-sitting club that Kristy runs.) "The Stones need shelter for some of their animals. The animals are too crowded in the little buildings on their property. So Mary Anne is asking her dad if they can take care of some of the animals for awhile." (Mary Anne lives in an old house with a barn on the property.)

She shifted the phone back so she could talk. "Yes, I am here," she said. "You can? Oh, great. Good. Okay, I will tell Mr. Stone."

Kristy hung up.

"What are you going to do?" I asked.

"Mr. Spier has said they can keep some of the Stones' animals, just temporarily," said Kristy. "Now we have to fix up their barn for the animals."

"Fix it up how?" I got a cookie to go with my juice.

"Well, they do not use their barn for anything now," said Kristy. "It needs to be cleaned out. We have to put down fresh hay. I am going to ask our friends in the Baby-sitters Club to help me."

"You forgot one thing," I said.

"What?"

"Me!" I said. "I will help too."

On Saturday morning Charlie drove Kristy and me to Mary Anne's. Mary Anne, her father, and her stepmother live in an old farmhouse near the edge of town. The house was fixed up, but the barn was not. I had been in it plenty of times. Usually it is a place for *people* to get together. Not animals.

"Gee," I said, looking at it. Stalls lined both sides, but they were cobwebby. Dusty bales of hay were lying around, but they would not be good for the animals to eat. They were too old.

Kristy pushed up the sleeves of her sweatshirt. "Let's get started, everyone! Mary Anne and I will move these old hay bales out of here. Claudia and Karen, you can start sweeping. Jessi, Mallory — once Claudia has swept out a few stalls, you can start laying out fresh hay and water."

Ha! And people think *I* am bossy! I found a broom and started sweeping.

It took us nearly all day to get the barn ready for the animals. We took a break at lunchtime. Mary Anne's stepmother fixed us all-natural turkey hot dogs on whole-wheat buns. They were okay.

We worked until almost dinnertime. Kristy walked through the barn and made an inspection. It looked great. The stalls were clean. There was fresh hay and water. There were also bags of sheep chow and goat chow, and oats for the horses. We were ready.

The very next day Charlie drove Kristy and me to Mary Anne's house again. We were there in time to help Mr. Stone deliver the animals. He had to make several trips. We put Ollie and Elvira into one big stall so they could keep each other company. General Sherman got his own stall. So did Ike. There were three more goats and two more grown-up sheep in other stalls.

"I sure do appreciate this," Mr. Stone told Mr. Spier. He wiped his forehead with his handkerchief. Moving animals is hard work. "They were getting mighty cramped in our little barn and in the greenhouse. I know they'll be happier here."

"It is no problem," said Mr. Spier. "We are happy to keep the animals for you, for awhile."

"We'll be making a decision very soon," said Mr. Stone. "One way or the other."

What did he mean by that? I wondered. He knew we were going to have a winter festival. Soon he would have enough money to rebuild his barn. Or . . . maybe he was unsure about that. Maybe he thought we would *not* make enough money for a new barn. I kicked the toe of my boot through the snow. We just had to raise enough money. We just *had* to.

In the meantime, at least I would not have to worry about Ollie anymore. He was all cozy in his new stall. And I would visit him whenever I could.

The Sleigh

Now that the animals were comfortable, it was time to take care of a very important item: the sleigh.

After school one day, Charlie, Sam, and I went to the Stones'. We found the sleigh in the back of their little barn. It was covered with dust and old hay and cobwebs.

"Yuck," said Charlie. "Well, let's get started."

With brooms and brushes we cleared off most of the mess. Then Mrs. Stone gave us buckets of hot water. We squirted in dish-washing liquid. With the hot, soapy water, we scrubbed that whole sleigh, inside and out. It was hot, messy work. Outside the barn it was snowing again and cold, but we were toasty warm.

You know what? When we were done, the sleigh looked better, but it did not look great. We all gazed at it. Then I sat down on a hay bale. I was hot and wet and tired. My clothes were filthy, and my hair had cob-webs in it. And looking at that sleigh made me want to cry.

It was clean, but that was all. It still looked old and worn out. The seats were split, and stuffing was coming out. The sides were scratched and rusty. The sleigh runners were dull. It did not look Christ-massy. It did not look fun. It did not look all jingle-bellsy.

"What are we going to do? It looks terri-ble," I wailed. "The festival is in ten days. We have already sold lots of tickets saying we will have fabulous sleigh rides, but our sleigh is not fabulous. It is yucky." I put my head down on my arms.

"Hey," said Sam. He patted my head. "It will be all right, just you wait."

"Yeah," said Charlie. "Now that it is clean, we can see what we are dealing with. Right, Sam?"

"Yes," said Sam. "Like, I can see that we need to paint the sides."

"I need to sand the runners and polish them, and wax them up for the snow," said Charlie.

"We need new seat covers," said Sam. "And Karen? You will have to make lots of decorations for the sleigh. The kind you are famous for."

I lifted my head. I sniffled and wiped my eyes. I looked at the sleigh and squinted. I could almost see it painted, with new seat covers and shiny runners. I could almost imagine my beautiful decorations. I looked at my two big brothers.

"Really?" I said. "Do you think it will be okay?"

Charlie smiled at me. "I think it will be gigundoly okay."

So that is what we did. Sam and Charlie painted the outside of the sleigh with shiny red paint. Once it was painted, it looked practically brand-new. Charlie sanded the rust off the runners. He painted the tops black, and waxed the undersides so they would glide smoothly over the snow.

Now for the seats. Elizabeth helped us find new fabric. It was in a red-and-green Christmas print. Together we tacked the new fabric to the old seats. I bounced on the front seat. It was pretty comfortable. Last of all we polished the metal trim on the sleigh. Now the sleigh had shiny brass fittings. I could see my face in them.

Then Andrew and David Michael and I went to work. We glued jingly gold bells onto wide red ribbon. We tied the red ribbons all over the sleigh. Daddy gave us a bunch of evergreen branches. We wove them into garlands and fastened the garlands onto the sleigh. It looked very beautiful. Last of all, Charlie rigged up a little battery pack. David Michael and I borrowed strings of tiny white lights from Daddy. We carefully fastened the white lights onto the garlands. The lights plugged into the battery pack.

We were done. Sam, Charlie, Elizabeth, David Michael, Andrew, and I stepped back to admire our work.

"It is truly beautiful," said Elizabeth.

"That is the best-looking sleigh I have ever seen," said David Michael.

"You better believe it," said Sam.

"I cannot wait to ride in it," said Charlie.

"It looks magical," said Andrew. "It looks like Santa's sleigh."

"Yes, it does," I agreed. I felt very happy. We had turned a yucky old worn-out sleigh into a beautiful Christmas sleigh. With the red paint and the bells and the garlands and the twinkly little lights, it looked just like something Santa would ride in. "But for goodness sake, do not tell Emily Michelle that!"

Karen's Christmas Tree

The next morning at breakfast Andrew said, "Everyone is worrying about the Stones' barn. Everyone is working on the winter festival. But no one is working on us."

"What do you mean, honey?" asked Elizabeth.

"It will be Christmas soon, right here in this house," said Andrew. "But we do not have any decorations. We do not have presents. We do not have a tree or Christmas lights."

I looked up from my waffle. Thank heavens Emily Michelle hadn't come downstairs yet.

"Andrew is right," said Kristy. "I am glad we have been helping the Stones. But we should make sure we are ready for our own Christmas."

"Thank you for reminding us, Andrew," said Daddy. "I know — I will stop working early today. Anyone who wants to go with me to pick out a Christmas tree, be ready at four o'clock."

"Yea!" said Andrew.

"Yea!" I said.

"And while you are gone, I will take out our decorations," said Nannie. "Emily Michelle will help me."

"Good," said Elizabeth. "Then tonight after dinner, we can all help decorate the house and the tree."

I smiled across the table at Andrew. He smiled back. I felt excited about *everything*.

"This one," I said, pointing. We were at the Christmas-tree lot. Andrew and David

Michael and I could not agree on which tree to buy. I wanted the very tallest one. Andrew wanted the very fattest one. David Michael wanted the one that was the darkest green.

"No, this one," said Andrew. He rubbed his mittened hands together. His breath came out as little puffs of smoke. We were getting cold.

"You guys, come see this one over here," said Daddy. He led us through rows and rows of Christmas trees. They smelled very fresh and green. Finally he stopped in front of a particular tree.

"I like this one," said Daddy. "It is not as tall as yours, Karen, and not as fat as yours, Andrew, and not even as green as yours, David Michael. But it has a beautiful shape. It looks just right to me."

I looked at it. Andrew looked at it. David Michael looked at it. We walked around the tree to inspect every side.

Finally we decided.

"It is just right," said David Michael.

"It is perfect," said Andrew.

"It is gigundoly perfect," I said.

"Good," said Daddy. "Now, let's take it home."

That night I wanted to skip dinner and start putting up Christmas decorations. But Nannie, Elizabeth, and Daddy all said I had to sit down and eat something. So I quickly wolfed down some chicken casserole. Then I sat, bouncing a little in my chair, until everyone else had finished.

"All right, Karen," said Daddy, wiping his mouth with his napkin. "I think we are ready."

"Great!" I cried. I leaped from my chair and ran to the living room. Daddy had put the tree in its stand, in front of the big living-room window. At night, when it was lit, people would be able to see our tree as they drove by.

Nannie had organized all our decorations.

Kristy and Sam put evergreen garlands on the staircase railings. Charlie and Daddy stood on ladders to put ornaments on the top of the tree. Andrew, Nannie, David Michael, and I put ornaments on the bottom of the tree. Elizabeth made hot chocolate. Then she put special Christmas candles on the mantels.

Emily Michelle was not helpful at all. She kept grabbing tree ornaments (breakable ones). I tried to help her put the Christmas elves on the very bottom branches of the tree, but she did not want to do that. She got in Daddy's way on the ladder, and pulled down one of Kristy's red ribbons.

"Emily," cried Kristy. "Please do not do that."

"Pwesants!" said Emily Michelle. "Santa!"

"Come here, sweetie," said Nannie. "I will give you some ornaments to put on the tree by yourself." She handed Emily some soft fabric ornaments. Emily grabbed a branch roughly, then cried out when the needles pricked her. The branch swung back, and a

52

glass ornament fell off and broke on the floor.

"Emily Michelle!" I cried. "You are being a pain!"

My little sister burst into tears.

"Karen, you do not have to snap at her," said Daddy.

"I am sorry," I said. Now Daddy and Elizabeth were upset with me. Emily was upset with me too. At the moment, I did not feel very Christmassy.

Dashing Through
the Snow

Later I apologized to Emily. She forgave me. I was feeling lots of Christmas spirit — and I just had to remind myself to feel some for Emily too.

The winter festival was going to take place four days before Christmas. Only one weekend was left before the festival, and there was still a lot to do.

Plus, I had not come up with a good idea for gifts for my two best friends. But I had not had much time to think about that. Now Christmas was just around the corner. I had to come up with something *soon*.

On Saturday morning, Hannie, Nancy, and I met Kristy and the other members of the Baby-sitters Club at the Stones' farm.

"Okay, everyone, listen up," Kristy said. "The sleigh rides will be on a circular route along these old cart tracks and through those woods." She pointed to the woods that bordered the Stones' property. "We need to make sure there is a clear path. We will mark that path with red ribbons and small lights. Okay?"

"Okay," we replied.

Marking the trail was hard work, but fun. We had bundled up extra warmly. Kristy and her friends stomped through the snow, looking for openings wide enough for the sleigh. They held branch cutters and hedge clippers. Sometimes they would trim a small branch that was in the way.

The Three Musketeers followed the older kids. We carried armfuls of red ribbons. We tied them to small trees on each side of the trail so that Charlie would be able to see which way to go. Later, Sam and Charlie would nail up strings of small lights along the trail.

"It will look like a magical forest," said Hannie as she tied a red ribbon.

"I cannot wait to take a sleigh ride," said Nancy. "Will there be warm blankets in the sleigh?"

"Yes." I nodded. "Plenty of warm blankets in the sleigh. And plenty of hot chocolate and spicy cider for afterward."

"I am so glad you thought of this, Karen," said Hannie.

"Thank you," I said. "I just hope that we will earn enough money for the Stones to rebuild their barn."

The next day we all trooped to the Stones' farm again. We set up areas for the snowman-building contest and the ice-sculpting contest. We marked the edges of the Stones' frozen pond so people could

ice-skate. My stepfather, Seth, and some of his carpenter friends were making booths. People in the booths would sell refreshments and tickets and homemade crafts. There would also be games, such as beanbag throwing and a ring toss.

Mrs. Stone came outside and offered us cookies and something warm to drink. "My goodness," she said, "I have never seen people work so hard. I cannot tell you how much we appreciate this."

"We are happy to do it," said Kristy.

"We are having fun," said Jessi Ramsey.

"It is all in the Christmas spirit," I said grandly.

As my friends and I ate our cookies, I thought again about presents for Hannie and Nancy. I did not have much money to spend. Could I learn to knit before Christmas? Maybe I could knit them scarves. Then I shook my head. There was no way I would have enough time to knit two scarves before Christmas. Even *I* knew that. What could I do, what could I do . . .

"Karen, what are you thinking about?" asked Hannie. "You are frowning so hard, your glasses are fogging up."

I giggled. My glasses were not really fogging up.

"Oh, I am just thinking about the festival," I said.

"It is going to be so much fun," said Nancy.

"I cannot wait," said Hannie.

I nodded. I was really looking forward to having fun at the festival, but I was also *not* looking forward to it. Because by the winter festival, Christmas would be only four days away. If I did not have great gifts for Hannie and Nancy by then, things would not be so merry after all.

Not Good Enough?

Later that week Daddy hosted a winter-festival meeting at the big house. Practically a million people came. Because it had all been my idea, I sat next to Daddy at the dining-room table. One by one people reported on what they had been doing. We already knew about some things. Other things were news to us. But it was the first time everyone had met together to talk about the festival.

"My friends and I have been selling tickets," Kristy told us. "We have sold almost two hundred tickets for ten dollars each. One ticket allows a person to enter all the contests and take one sleigh ride. Plus we will be selling tickets at the door."

Daddy wrote down the numbers in a notebook.

Mrs. Epstein from the library board stood up next. "Members of the library board will be donating the refreshments," she said. "We will have hot chocolate, hot apple cider, sodas, coffee, and tea. We will also have sandwiches, doughnuts, caramel popcorn, cookies, cakes, pies, and hot soup. And we will be selling whole cakes, pies, and breads at our library booth."

"That is great," said Daddy. He wrote down all that information. "Let me see, if everyone buys at least one food item, and over two hundred people come . . ." He took out his calculator and added some figures. "Good. The refreshments will be a terrific source of income. Thank you."

Mrs. Epstein sat down.

Mr. Cookson, who works with Elizabeth at her ad agency, stood up. "We have been collecting cash donations at our office," he said. "We have collected over four hundred dollars so far."

"Wonderful," said Daddy. He wrote it down.

"My school has collected money too," said David Michael. "We have one hundred and twenty-seven dollars here."

"That's great," said Daddy.

Hundreds and hundreds of dollars! I could not believe how much money people had donated. I bet the Stones would have enough money to build a humongous, fancy barn, and have some money left over. Maybe they would buy more animals to fill up the new barn.

Daddy was using his calculator again. He cleared his throat. "I estimate that our final figure will be about five thousand dollars, give or take a couple hundred," he said.

"That will be a wonderful gift to the Stones. Thank you all for being so generous and for working so hard."

Everyone cheered and clapped their hands.

Daddy held up his hand. "However, I am sad to report that to rebuild their barn, the Stones will probably need almost twice that much."

Boo and bullfrogs. I could not believe that even with all that money, the Stones might need even more.

"Do you mean they will not be able to rebuild their barn?" I cried.

"Well," said Daddy. "They will need to find more funds somewhere. Or maybe more people will show up at the winter festival than we expect. I do not know."

I slumped down in my chair. This was terrible.

"Do not worry, Karen," said Kristy. "We do not know what will happen. Maybe everyone will buy tons of refreshments.

Maybe people from other towns will show up. It could still turn out all right. Try not to get upset."

"I will try," I said. "But if the Stones cannot rebuild their barn, and Mary Anne's daddy cannot keep the animals in his barn, then the Stones might lose Ollie forever."

Let the Festival Begin!

"I thought today would never come!" I told Moosie the following Sunday morning. (Moosie is my stuffed cat.)

Today was the day of the winter festival. It would not start until three o'clock in the afternoon, but I had something else very important to do today. I cannot tell you what it was (yet), but I will give you two hints: It was an art project, and it was for Hannie and Nancy.

* * *

My whole big-house family arrived early at the Stones' farm. Mr. and Mrs. Stone were waiting for us.

"We are so excited," said Mrs. Stone. "This is going to be so much fun."

"Maybe we should do this every year," said Mr. Stone. "Whether our barn burns down or not." He laughed.

There were all sorts of last-minute details that I had to take care of. Because I had thought up the winter festival, it was up to me to make sure everything was perfect. This is what I had to do:

1) Check all the booths to make sure they were ready. (They were.)

2) See if the pond was ready for ice-skating. (It was.)

3) Check to make sure Kristy was selling tickets at the gate. (She was.)

Finally I looked over the snowman-building area. It was marked with a big poster. Good. So was the ice-sculpting place. And a bunch of gigundo blocks of ice were standing around. People would use hammers and chisels to make sculptures out of the ice. They would be beautiful when they were done.

"Karen!" Elizabeth called. "People are starting to arrive."

I ran to the entrance gate. One of my jobs was to greet people as they arrived. (I had given myself this job. I knew I would be good at it.)

"Hello, hello!" I called. Guess what. The very first people to arrive were my teacher, Ms. Colman, her husband, Mr. Simmons, and their baby daughter, Jane. "Welcome to the winter festival!" I said.

"Thank you," said Ms. Colman and Mr. Simmons. (Jane did not say thank you. She is just a baby. She does not talk yet.)

"Make yourself at home," I said, waving my hand toward the Stones' farm. "There is plenty of fun to be had." I had read that phrase in a book. I thought it sounded good.

"All right, we will," said Mr. Simmons.

"Be sure to have some refreshments," I reminded them. I put my hand to one side of

my mouth. "They cost extra," I whispered.

"I understand," said Mr. Simmons.

They smiled at me and headed toward the booths. I wanted to see what they would do first, but I could not, because more people were arriving.

"Hello, hello!" I cried. "Welcome to the winter festival! Please come in. There is plenty of fun to be had!"

I greeted people until I felt I was about to drop. My voice was hoarse from talking so much. I felt hungry and thirsty. Mrs. Stone said she would be happy to greet people for awhile.

I bought a cup of hot apple cider with my own money. It was another way to help the Stones, and the cider felt so good going down! After a cup of delicious soup, I ate two doughnuts for dessert. Then I felt much better. I was ready to put my plan into action.

First I found Kristy. She was taking a break from selling tickets. "Hundreds of people have come, Karen," she said happily.

"The more, the merrier," I said. "Kristy, I need your help for a moment."

I told Kristy what I needed her to do.

"That is a great idea, Karen," said Kristy. "I know Hannie and Nancy will really like that gift."

"Thank you," I said. "Then I will see you later, okay? I will give you a signal."

"Okay," said Kristy.

I looked around the Stones' farm. It was starting to get dark. There were people everywhere. The good news was that it looked like our winter festival would be a huge success. The bad news was that even if it were a huge success, it still might not be good enough.

Snowmen

At twilight Charlie organized the first sleigh ride. (Twilight is when it is not exactly day, and not exactly night. Twilight does not last very long.) The sleigh could hold four people besides the driver. A family with two children was first in line. Charlie seated them in the sleigh and covered their laps with blankets. Then he climbed into the driver's seat and picked up the reins.

"Hi, General Sherman!" he said. "Giddyup!" General Sherman started off, pulling the sleigh easily over the hard-packed snow.

Hannie and Nancy were standing next to me.

"I cannot wait until it is my turn," said Nancy.

"Me neither," I said.

"But first there is the snowman-building contest," said Hannie. "And I have signed us up for it."

The contest was taking place in a small open field behind the burned-down barn. Since it was now dark, Mr. Stone turned on the floodlights that had been set up all over the farm.

Besides us, Bobby Gianelli and Chris Lamar from Ms. Colman's class had signed up for the contest. And so had Claudia, Kristy's friend. Several grown-ups had signed up also.

"Places, everyone," called Mr. Stone. He and Mrs. Stone were going to be the judges.

We ran to a nice open spot where the snow was very deep. The three of us had decided to build a large snowbunny. First we rolled a gigundo ball of snow for the bottom. Then a medium-size ball for the middle. Hannie and I lifted it into place. Then we made a smaller ball for the bunny's head. Now the snowbunny was almost as tall as we were.

The ears were difficult. It was hard to pack snow into a long, pointy shape. We did the best we could, but they did not really look much like a bunny's ears. (I should know. I used to have a bunny. Her name was Princess Cleopatra.)

We made whiskers out of small twigs. Nancy found two rocks for the eyes and one for the nose. There! Our bunny was complete.

"This is a great snowbunny," Nancy said.

"It is a terrific snowbunny," I said. "And it is the only one."

We had to wait for everyone to finish before the judges gave out ribbons.

One man had made a snow house. Bobby and Chris had made the biggest snowman they could. He looked just like Frosty the Snowman. Claudia had made a very fancy snowwoman. She was wearing snow pearls around her neck. Someone else had made a snowfrog. Another team had made a beautiful snow angel. (I liked that one the best. After our bunny, I mean.)

Mr. and Mrs. Stone looked at each snow sculpture. Hannie and Nancy and I held hands. I felt nervous but excited. I love contests! Other people came to watch the judging. I saw Kristy standing with her camera. I winked at her, and she winked back.

Well, the first-prize blue ribbon went to the beautiful snow angel. The second-prize red ribbon went to . . . the Three Musketeers! And Claudia won third prize with her snowwoman.

"Yes!" Hannie cried.

Nancy and I jumped up and down and hugged each other.

The three of us held on to the ribbon and stood in front of our snowbunny while Kristy took our picture.

74

Kristy said, "Say macaroni and —"

"Cheese!" we shouted. *Click.*

We decided to have hot cider to celebrate. Then Daddy announced that it was time for the ice-sculpting contest.

"Let's hurry!" I said.

Jack Frost

The ice-sculpting contest was held in the small barn. Inside several very large blocks of ice were set on stands. Hannie and Nancy and I found good places to sit (on a hay bale) and we settled in to watch.

Only grown-ups had signed up for this. It is harder than making a snowman. Each person had a small hammer and some chisels. Carefully they set the chisels against their huge blocks of ice and chipped away. It took a long time.

Outside, in the dark, tiny white lights lit

Charlie's way through the woods. I kept hearing the jingling jingle bells on the sleigh. They sounded loud when Charlie pulled up to get more people, and then they faded as he drove away. Everywhere people were laughing and eating and playing in the snow. I was having a good time too, but I could not help worrying about whether the Stones would be able to rebuild their barn.

"There you are," said Kristy. She sat down next to us. "Wow, look at that one." She pointed to one ice sculpture.

I nodded. "I think he will win," I said.

The man in front of us was carving a statue of Jack Frost. It looked like a small elf with a pointed hat and a little beard. His shoes were curled up at the toes. It was amazing.

Several people had already dropped out of the contest because they had broken their ice into little bits by mistake. Only a few people were left.

"Kristy," I whispered in her ear.

She leaned down.

"What if the Stones cannot rebuild their barn?" I said softly. "They will have to sell their animals. Maybe they will move away forever. They will be sad. And we will never have farm camp again."

"Oh, do not worry about it," Kristy said airily. "Everything will be all right. You will see."

I looked at her. "How do you know everything will be all right?" I asked. "We might not earn enough money. Maybe not enough people are here. Maybe the Stones —"

"It will be okay, Karen," Kristy said. "I am sure."

I did not know how she could say that. But she was my big sister. She was not wrong very often.

Soon the contest was over. A man from the library board was the judge. He gave the first prize to the man who had made Jack Frost. We all cheered and clapped. The second prize went to a lady who had carved a log out of ice. Third prize was awarded to a small ice dog.

"Maybe next year I will try the ice-sculpting contest," I said as we headed outside again. "I will practice on ice cubes at home."

"Good idea," said Nancy. "Maybe you could make an ice mermaid or an ice unicorn."

"Or an ice castle," said Hannie.

"Those are good ideas," I said. "I will be ready for the contest next year."

"Speaking of ice," said Nancy. "We have not been ice-skating yet. Did you bring your skates?"

I nodded. "Daddy has them."

"Well, what are we waiting for?" asked Nancy.

"I will meet you guys at the pond," I said. Then I ran to find Daddy. Snowbunnies, Jack Frost, ice-skating . . . The winter festival was even more fun than I had thought it would be!

Merry Christmas, Mrs. Stone

Skating at night had been gigundoly fun. Now all the contests and games were over, and people gathered around the refreshment booths. Mrs. Stone passed out small white candles. Nancy, Hannie, and I were each allowed to have one. (I had to share mine with Andrew.) When all the candles were lit, they looked very beautiful.

"Deck the halls with boughs of holly," I sang. "Fa la la la la, la la la la. 'Tis the season to be jolly . . ." Everyone joined in to sing Christmas carols together. It sounded wonderful to hear us singing in that cold air. In the distance, the sleigh's jingle bells jingled.

Hannie and Nancy smiled at me, and I smiled back. We sang more carols. It was very special and Christmassy, but I felt sad. I bet that we had not earned enough money for the Stones' new barn, no matter what Kristy had said.

Next to me, Andrew started singing his favorite Christmas song. "Rudolph, the red-nosed reindeer . . ."

So we all started singing that.

After we had sung practically all the holiday songs we knew, Daddy stepped up onto a box and clapped his hands for attention.

"Good evening, everyone," he said. "I hope you have all had a good time at the first annual Stoneybrook Winter Festival."

People clapped and cheered.

"As you know, we did not hold this festival just for fun," said Daddy, "although it has been lots of fun. But this festival was our way of trying to help our friends Mr. and Mrs. Stone."

We clapped again.

"Over the years," continued Daddy, "the Stones have been good friends and neighbors to all of us, and to our children. We would hate to lose them. I hope we will not have to. Since my daughter Karen thought up the winter-festival plan, I would like her to present this check to Mr. and Mrs. Stone."

Everyone clapped again. (Except me. It is not polite to clap for yourself.) I walked through the crowd and climbed up on the box next to Daddy. He handed me a check. I tried to smile, although I did not feel like it. All of our hard work was for nothing. The Stones would not have a merry Christmas. They would move away. I would lose Ollie and Elvira and all the other animals.

Mr. and Mrs. Stone came forward. Mrs. Stone had to wipe her eyes several times.

I held out the check. "This is for you. Merry Christmas from all of us," I said.

"Oh, thank you, Karen," said Mrs. Stone.

"Words are not enough to thank you, and everyone else here, for what you have done. But they are all we can offer just now."

Mr. Stone put his arm around her, and they hugged. Mrs. Stone sniffled. Then she and Mr. Stone looked at the check. Their eyes widened. They stared at each other, and then at me, and then at Daddy.

"Why, this is . . ." said Mr. Stone.

"This is exactly what we need to rebuild the barn!" said Mrs. Stone.

My mouth dropped open. I looked at Daddy.

He smiled. "I guess we took in more tonight than we had expected," he said.

"But how?" I said. "That is almost twice as much as we thought."

Daddy shrugged.

"Thank you, thank you!" the Stones cried. First they hugged me, then Daddy, then anyone else they could get their hands on. Mrs. Stone was crying, and Mr. Stone was shaking hands left and right.

I jumped off the box and went back to Hannie, Nancy, and Andrew.

"I do not know how that happened," I said. "Somehow we earned enough money."

"Maybe Santa Claus donated some money too," said Andrew.

"Santa!" cried Emily Michelle. She bounced in Nannie's arms. "Santa!"

"It is a Christmas mystery," I said. "A wonderful one."

Karen's Sleigh Ride

"It is getting late, Karen," said Elizabeth. "If you are going to take a sleigh ride, you better do it now."

"Okay!" I said. "Who will go with me?"

"I will," said Kristy.

"Me too," said Daddy.

"Me, me!" shouted Andrew.

The four of us climbed into the sleigh. Charlie tucked warm blankets over our laps.

"Everyone ready?" he asked.

"Ready!" I said.

Charlie clucked his tongue at General Sherman, and we set off.

Well, if you have never been on a sleigh ride, you do not know how gigundoly fabulous it can be. It was dark outside, and cold, but we were toasty warm. The sleigh bells jingled, and the little white lights strung through the trees made them look like an enchanted forest.

Best of all, I knew I did not have to worry about the Stones anymore. They were going to stay. Their animals were going to stay. Everything would be all right.

General Sherman knew the sleigh ride path so well by now that Charlie did not have to do very much. The sleigh slid smoothly over the snow. I leaned my head on Daddy's shoulder, and he put his arm around me on one side, and Andrew on the other.

I thought that this might just be the very best Christmas ever.

"Dashing through the snow," I sang, "in a

one-horse open sleigh, o'er the fields we go . . ."

"Laughing all the way!" Kristy sang.

"Bells on bobtails ring," sang Daddy, "making spirits bright . . ."

"Oh, what fun it is to ride and sing," sang Andrew.

"A sleighing song tonight! Hey!"

The Perfect End to a Perfect Day

It was way past my bedtime. It was a good thing I did not have school the next day. (I had the whole next week off for our winter vacation.)

Almost everyone had left the winter festival. Only a few people were there, besides my family. We were all helping to clean up and pack things away.

David Michael and I were walking around the farmyard, picking up trash. Kristy was collecting signs and posters. Daddy and Elizabeth were helping to take down the booths. Sam and Charlie were removing decorations. A few people were gathering up their trays and punch bowls and other things they had brought to the festival.

Close by, Nannie was rocking Emily Michelle in her arms.

"Mrs. Taylor, wouldn't you rather take her inside?" asked Mrs. Stone. (Mrs. Taylor is Nannie.) "We have a nice rocking chair in the living room."

"Oh, no, thank you," said Nannie. "As soon as I took her coat off and got her settled down, it would be time to bundle her back up again. But thank you anyway."

Emily wriggled in Nannie's arms. "Santa's sway!" she cried. Her eyes were shut, and she was almost asleep.

"Shh," Nannie soothed her. Nannie walked around slowly, trying to lull Emily to sleep.

Daddy had pulled up our station wagon and opened the back.

"Karen, could you please put these things in the car for me?" asked Elizabeth. She handed me some bags of paper plates and napkins.

"Sure," I said. Inside the car, Andrew was stretched across one of the seats, covered with a blanket. He was sound asleep. I wished I could curl up next to him. But I was not a little kid like he was. I needed to help Daddy and Elizabeth and everyone else.

I leaned into the car and pushed the bag of stuff way in the back.

"Well, I am so glad the Stones will be able to rebuild," I heard someone say.

"Yes, thanks to Watson Brewer," someone else said.

I stayed very still. Didn't they mean thanks to *Karen* Brewer? I was the one who came up with the winter-festival idea.

"What do you mean?" asked the first person.

"Didn't you know? He donated the rest of the money they needed. The proceeds from tonight were not enough," said the second person. "So Watson made up the difference with his own money."

"Oh. How generous of him!"

"Yes . . . " Their voices faded away as they walked on.

I sat on the bumper of the car for a moment. So that was how we had been able to give the Stones that big check. No wonder Kristy had never been as worried about it as I had been. She had known that Daddy was going to pitch in so that the Stones could rebuild their barn.

Even though I was very tired, I felt gigundoly happy. Those people had been right: Daddy was generous. I was proud of him. I decided I would keep his secret. If anyone asked me, I would say that the extra money must have come from Santa Claus.

"There you are, honey," said Elizabeth, from behind me. "I think we are about done. Could you please wake Andrew and make sure he is buckled in? I know you are ready to go home and go to bed." She smoothed my hair off my forehead.

"Yes. I am very tired," I said. "But I am happy too. It was a great winter festival."

Elizabeth smiled. "Yes, there was plenty of fun to be had," she said. "And it was all thanks to you."

"Not *all* of it," I said, thinking of Daddy.

Chill Out, Emily Michelle

"**W**ant wide!" Emily Michelle yelled. "Want sway!" She kicked the sides of her high chair and squirmed to get down. "No lunch!"

"You do not have to eat lunch," said Nannie firmly. "But you do have to sit in your high chair and keep us company for awhile. When we are done, you may get down."

Andrew looked at me across the kitchen table. He rolled his eyes. I shrugged, and took another bite of my sandwich. Emily Michelle had been a pain all morning long.

"I cannot believe Christmas is still three whole days away," Andrew said. "I do not know if I can wait that long."

"Me neither," said David Michael. "Time is crawling by so slowly."

"I am glad I have three more days to get ready," I said. "I still have a lot to do. I have to wrap my presents, and get Hannie's and Nancy's presents ready."

"Pwesants!" cried Emily Michelle. "Pwesants!" She burst into tears. Nannie tried to soothe her.

"Wasn't Hanukkah last week?" Kristy asked. She had to raise her voice to be heard over Emily.

"Yes," I said. "But Nancy said we could exchange presents closer to Christmas, because I was not ready last week."

"Will you help me wrap my presents, Karen?" asked Andrew. "I am not a very good wrapper."

"Yes," I said. "But first I think I will go to my room for a little peace and quiet." I gave Emily Michelle a Look.

But up in my room, I did not find peace and quiet. What I found was a mess! My dresser drawers had been dumped out on the floor. My closet door was open. All my shoes had been thrown around. Not only that, but some of my very special things had been taken off their shelves: my unicorn statue, an angel from my angel collection, and the friendship bracelet I had made at pony camp.

Only one person in the house would have done this. I stomped out into the hall. I stomped down the stairs. I stomped around until I found the culprit in the family room.

"Emily Michelle!" I shouted.

She was sitting on the floor, playing with a puzzle. She jumped when she heard my voice.

"I cannot believe what you did!" I said. "You wrecked my room! You have been very naughty! Naughty, naughty, naughty!"

Emily stared at me with her big black eyes. Then her face crumpled and her mouth opened.

"Waaaahhhhhh!" she cried. Fat tears rolled down her cheeks.

"Why did you do that?" I said, frowning at her. "You have your own things in your own room."

"Pwesants!" Emily Michelle sobbed. "Want Santa! Want pwesants!"

Ohhhh. Suddenly I thought I understood. We had been talking about Christmas and Santa Claus all month. And we all knew about Christmas. But Emily Michelle was just a toddler. She did not understand it the way the rest of us did. So all month she had been waiting for presents and for Santa Claus. She did not understand why they had not come yet. Finally she had searched my room, looking for them.

"Come here, Emily," I said. I sat down on the floor and pulled her onto my lap. She was sobbing and rubbing her eyes with her fists.

"I am sorry I yelled at you," I said. I patted her hair. "I was angry about my room. But do not worry about it. Now listen. I am

going to explain to you about Christmas, and about Santa Claus. We will talk about it until you are sure you understand. Okay?"

"Okay." Emily Michelle sniffled and snuggled up closer.

"Okay. Now. A long time ago . . ." I began.

With Love from Santa's Elf

That night, at dinnertime, Emily Michelle found a small gift on the tray of her high chair. Her eyes opened wide, and she started hopping up and down.

"Pwesant!" she cried, clapping her hands.

Nannie put her in her high chair, and Emily Michelle tore off the wrapping. Nannie took the card and read it for her.

"It says, 'Three more days until Christmas! With love to Emily Michelle from one of Santa's elves,' " said Nannie.

"What did Santa's elf give you, Emily?" asked Andrew.

"Ball!" she said, holding it up.

I had taken one of Daddy's tennis balls (I had asked him first) and written a big E.M. on it. It was a little present, but Emily looked very happy.

"Lucky Emily," said Nannie. "You have your very own tennis ball."

Emily beamed.

I smiled to myself as I took a dinner roll from the basket.

"Look," I said. "This is where we are now. This is Christmas, two days away." I pointed on the calendar to show Emily Michelle what I was talking about. "This is today. That is tomorrow. And the very next day is Christmas. Get it?"

Emily nodded solemnly. I did not know if she really did get it, but I was trying.

My little sister patted her hair. "Pwesent," she said. "Santa's eff."

"Yes," I said. "Santa's elf brought you a barrette today." She seemed happy, wearing my barrette with the little wooden tiger on it. I knew I would not miss it.

"Merry Christmas Eve!" said Hannie. She stomped her boots to shake the snow off.

"Merry Christmas Eve," I said. "Nancy will be here soon. Come on up to my room."

I could not believe that the very next day would be Christmas. All morning I had felt tingly and excited. I was sure I would not be able to sleep a wink tonight. But at least I was ready for the big day. I had asked Hannie and Nancy to come over to celebrate the holidays with me. Their gifts were waiting for them.

A few minutes later the doorbell rang, and then we heard Nancy running up the stairs.

"Hi," she said. "Merry Christmas Eve."

"Thank you," I said. "Happy late Hanukkah."

"Should we open our presents now?" asked Hannie.

"Wait," I said. "I have this all planned. First, a special snack."

I pulled out a plate of cookies and three cups of punch that I had hidden under my bed. (We are not really supposed to eat in our bedrooms. But Elizabeth had said it was okay, since it was Christmas Eve.)

Hannie and Nancy each took a cookie and a cup of punch.

I raised my cup in a toast. "I would like to make a toast to my two best friends," I said. "You helped me with the winter festival. You are always there for me. You laugh at my jokes. You will always be my two best friends. Merry Christmas. And Happy Hanukkah."

"Merry Christmas," said Hannie.

"Merry Christmas," said Nancy.

We all clinked cups and took a sip.

"Now, presents!" said Hannie. "You each get two things."

"Two? Wow," said Nancy.

We opened our gifts. Hannie had given us each a brand-new box of sidewalk chalk and a cool pair of shoelaces.

"See?" said Hannie. "The laces glow in the dark. So if you suddenly had to put your shoes on in the middle of the night, you would be able to find them, no problem."

"These are so cool," I said. "I will put them on my sneakers right away."

"I need new sidewalk chalk," said Nancy. "As soon as the snow melts, we can make new hopscotches on the driveway."

Hannie smiled at us.

"Here are my presents to you," said Nancy. She handed us each a very small package.

"Lip gloss!" I said. "Oh my gosh."

"I have some myself too," said Nancy. "On one side it is cherry, and on the other side it is plain."

I put some on right away. "Cherry! Thanks, Nancy. This is a great present."

My gifts for Hannie and Nancy were hidden in my desk drawer. I took them out.

"This is so we'll always remember the Three Musketeers," I said. I handed them each a square, flat package. They opened them.

"Perfect!" said Hannie with a smile. She held it up.

Remember when Kristy took a picture of the three of us after we won second place in the snowman-building contest at the winter festival? I had asked Daddy to have two copies made. And my art project, the morning of the festival, was making picture frames out of cardboard. I had decorated the frames by gluing on sprinkles and foil stars. I had also used holiday stickers. Hannie's was red, and Nancy's was blue.

"It is beautiful, Karen," said Nancy. "It is a great present."

"I will put it on my desk at home," said Hannie.

We all smiled at each other with our shiny lips.

Tap, tap. My door opened and Emily Michelle poked her head in.

"Come on in," I said. "Look! Santa's elf left some cookies for you."

My little sister ran in happily. She picked up a cookie. "Cwismas!" she said.

"Merry Christmas Eve, Emily," I said. "It is going to be a wonderful Christmas."

L. GODWIN

About the Author

ANN M. MARTIN lives in New York City and loves animals, especially cats. She has two cats of her own, Gussie and Woody.

Other books by Ann M. Martin that you might enjoy are *Stage Fright*; *Me and Katie (the Pest)*; and the books in *The Baby-sitters Club* series.

Ann likes ice cream and *I Love Lucy*. And she has her own little sister, whose name is Jane.

Little Sister

Don't miss #93

KAREN'S COOKING CONTEST

"One pound of chocolate," I wrote. I wanted to finish copying it before Nannie got home. Nannie would be so surprised to see her recipe for Chocolate Magic in our celebrity cookbook, I told myself. She would be the only person who was not a real celebrity. She would probably be very flattered, I decided. I did not listen to the voice in my head that reminded me that Nannie wanted the recipe to be secret. I was just too desperate.

I finished copying the recipe really fast. Then I snuck downstairs and put it back in Nannie's recipe box. There! Now I was all set.

BABY·SITTERS™
Little Sister

by Ann M. Martin
author of The Baby-sitters Club®

More Titles... ➡

LITTLE 🍎 APPLE®

Here are some of our favorite Little Apples.

There are fun times ahead with kids just like you in Little Apple books! Once you take a bite out of a Little Apple—you'll want to read more!

Reading Excitement for Kids with BIG Appetites!

☐ NA45899-X **Amber Brown Is Not a Crayon**
Paula Danziger $2.99

☐ NA93425-2 **Amber Brown Goes Fourth**
Paula Danziger $2.99

☐ NA50207-7 **You Can't Eat Your Chicken Pox, Amber Brown**
Paula Danziger $2.99

☐ NA42833-0 **Catwings** Ursula K. LeGuin $2.95

☐ NA42832-2 **Catwings Return** Ursula K. LeGuin $3.50

☐ NA41821-1 **Class Clown** Johanna Hurwitz $2.99

☐ NA42400-9 **Five True Horse Stories**
Margaret Davidson $2.99

☐ NA43868-9 **The Haunting of Grade Three**
Grace Maccarone $2.99

☐ NA40966-2 **Rent a Third Grader** B.B. Hiller $2.99

☐ NA41944-7 **The Return of the Third Grade Ghost Hunters**
Grace Maccarone $2.99

☐ NA42031-3 **Teacher's Pet** Johanna Hurwitz $3.50

Available wherever you buy books...or use the coupon below.

SCHOLASTIC INC., P.O. Box 7502, 2931 East McCarty Street, Jefferson City, MO 65102

Please send me the books I have checked above. I am enclosing $ _____ (please add $2.00 to cover shipping and handling). Send check or money order—no cash or C.O.D.s please.

Name_____

Address_____

City_____ State/Zip_____

Please allow four to six weeks for delivery. Offer good in the U.S.A. only. Sorry, mail orders are not available to residents of Canada. Prices subject to change.   LA996